book design by KEITH GRIFFIN

3-13-01

To 2 of my most precious grandchildren. Read & enjoy! Remember I love you very, very much.

Love
Papa
Griffin

This Book is
Dedicated to:

*Rachael & Kenny H Griffin*
child's name

and to all the other children who help us to see and feel the magic in our world. And also to my parents, whose love and wisdom have given me flight.

**MSS**

*Mary Sue Stevens*

Published by Dancing Toad
5109 Washburn Ave South
Minneapolis, Minnesota 55410 USA

Text copyright © 2000 Dancing Toad
Illustration copyright © 2000 Heather Holland

First Printing: November, 2000

Story written by Mary Sue Stevens
Illustrations by Heather Holland
Cover & Book design by Keith Griffin

ISBN # 0-9705625-0-0

A special thanks to The College of Visual Arts in St. Paul, Minnesota for allowing us to use their printing presses to make magic.

Printed and bound in the U.S.A
Ambassador Press, Minneapolis

*Heather Holland*
HH 2000

# The Magic Christmas Tree

magic words by
MARY SUE STEVENS

magic pictures by
HEATHER HOLLAND

Hana sat at the window of the tiny cabin in her boots, coat, and mittens watching for her father. Outside, the snowflakes grew **thicker** and **thicker** and the sun sank lower and lower beyond the forest trees.

While she waited,

her warm breath clouded the window, so she took off her mittens and drew FUNNY animals. Just as she was finishing the ears of a rabbit, the door swung open and in walked her rosy-cheeked father.

Hana ran to hug him. "Father," she pleaded, "can we still go find our tree tonight, please?"

By this time the sun had completely disappeared into the forest and the

MOON was just beginning to cast a bright, warm glow onto the snow.

Hana's father knew how much she loved the trees in the forest and how excited she was to have one inside to smell, touch, and decorate. He just couldn't say no.

Out the door they went and, after stopping by the woodshed to grab a saw, they headed off into the snowy forest to search for the perfect tree.

As they walked along, Hana and her father made up a song about the tree they hoped to find:

We are off into the woods to find a tree.
With the moon's bright
W

...ve are able to see.

...search and search to find the right one.

We will decorate it and wait for Christmas to come.

They had not walked far before Hana cried, "Look!" And there, brightly lit by a moon-beam, was the most beautiful little tree Hana had ever seen. "Father I know it is small, but it is so beautiful, this is the perfect tree. Please, father, can we have this one for our Christmas tree?"

The tree was so small, that after only a few strokes with the saw, it fell gently onto its side in the soft snow. Hana's father picked up the little tree with one hand, swung it over his shoulder, and carried it like that all the way back through the glistening forest.

Once inside, Hana's Father placed the little tree in a bucket filled with fresh water. Then he slid the tree between the stone fireplace and the oak rocking chair so Hana could see it from the dinner table.

All through dinner Hana talked about how she would decorate the little tree first thing in the morning. It was so small she would have to use the tiniest ornaments she had collected from the forest. The little tree made Hana so happy, that she believed this would be the best Christmas ever.

By the time Hana and her father were done with dinner, the M O O N had moved from one window to the other.

And after Hana yawned a third time, her father said it was tim for bed.

ladder...
up the
climbed
Hana

to her room. As she put
on her pajamas she
noticed how BIG and
bright the stars were.
She felt a chill,
hopped quickly
into bed, and
waited for her
father to
come tuck
her in.

She was almost asleep when her Father's head popped up into the room. He sat on the edge of the bed, just like he did every night, and arranged the covers snugly around her. As he tucked her in, he told Hana to remember to give thanks to the little tree because it was a special gift from the forest.

Hana fell into a deep sleep and began dreaming about decorating the little tree. Her father kissed her on the forehead and then climbed down the ladder.

Before Hana's father went to bed,
he glanced over at the little tree
and smiled. As the cabin grew
quiet, something magical began to
happen. The little tree began to
*quiver and shake.*

It stretched and stretched with
all its branches, pushing itself
higher and higher until it
pushed its way through
the round window in
Hana's room.

Still it kept going further and further up, up into the night sky.

When the tree finally stopped growing, it was far, far up in the sky, past the clouds, beyond the MOON, deep into the night sky, with its enormous branches reaching for the stars. And there among the stars, it began to turn and sway rocking back and forth, back and forth. As the tree danced and turned, stars became caught in its waving branches.

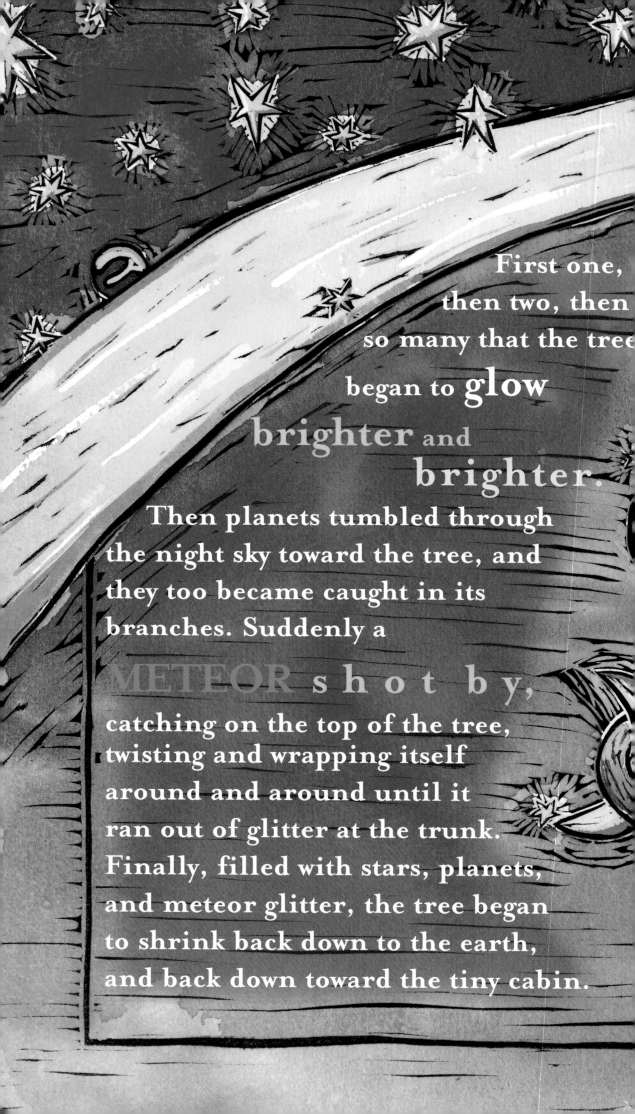

First one,
then two, then
so many that the tree
began to glow
brighter and
brighter.
Then planets tumbled through
the night sky toward the tree, and
they too became caught in its
branches. Suddenly a
METEOR shot by,
catching on the top of the tree,
twisting and wrapping itself
around and around until it
ran out of glitter at the trunk.
Finally, filled with stars, planets,
and meteor glitter, the tree began
to shrink back down to the earth,
and back down toward the tiny cabin.

Animals from the forest gathered around in awe of its beauty and brought gifts of their own to hang in its glowing branches.

Many colorful beetles climbed over the meteor glitter and made squiggly patterns on the planets with their feet and antennae. Luna moths fluttered around the tree leaving yellow and blue dust on the tips of needles.

Several **red** squirrels brought bright **berries** and wrapped them in and around the swaying limbs.

Two doves
wove a nest
near the treetop
and filled it
with fluffy
white feathers
and three
golden eggs.

Deer, raccoons, wolves, rabbits, and bears formed a circle around the CABIN holding onto each other's paws and hooves, laughing and dancing as the tree was decorated.

After the last luna moth flew off, the tree was so full of such marvelous gifts and glitter, that it barely squeezed back into the cabin through the small round window, before settling peacefully into its place once again.

The glow from the beautifully-decorated tree was so radiant that the whole cabin was lit and filled with magical warmth.

Hana was awakened by this warmth on her cheeks and eyelids, and at first she thought that the sun had found its way through a crack in the wall. But when she opened her eyes, she realized that the light was coming from

inSIDE the cabin!

She quickly climbed d o w n the ladder following the g l o w. And as she turned around she gasped, for the little tree stood just where she and her father had left it, but something wondrous and magical had happened while she was dreaming.

The little tree now twinkled and glowed with the most wonderful gifts from the sky and the forest. Hana wrapped her arms around the tree and said,

"Thank you beautiful little tree."

The tree twinkled back with such magical warmth that Hana could feel its love.

Mary Sue Stevens

Mary Sue Stevens has spent fifteen years professionally teaching and learning from children. These years of experience and her love of nature have led her to the writing of her first children's book, *The Magic Christmas Tree*. She is currently working on several other children's books and a line of multi-cultural toys. She lives in Minneapolis with her husband Jeff Aldrich.

dancing
toad
BOOKS

**Heather Holland & Keith Griffin**

Living in Minneapolis, along with their daughter, Holland (who has been a great audience to test the magic), this married team has had the privilege of creating their first children's book together. Heather, the illustrator, and Keith, the designer, find it easy to work together and get inspiration from each other. Influenced by their daughter, they look forward to creating more magic for children together. :)